Trey Parker's
Cannibal!

The Musical

Book, Music, and Lyrics
New Cannibal Society

SAMUELFRENCH.COM
SAMUELFRENCH-LONDON.CO.UK

FOR PRODUCTION ENQUIRIES

UNITED STATES AND CANADA
Info@SamuelFrench.com
1-866-598-8449

UNITED KINGDOM AND EUROPE
Plays@SamuelFrench-London.co.uk
020-7255-4302

Each title is subject to availability from Samuel French, depending upon country of performance. Please be aware that *TREY PARKER'S CANNIBAL! THE MUSICAL* may not be licensed by Samuel French in your territory. Professional and amateur producers should contact the nearest Samuel French office or licensing partner to verify availability.

MUSIC USE NOTE

Licensees are solely responsible for obtaining formal written permission from copyright owners to use copyrighted music in the performance of this play and are strongly cautioned to do so. If no such permission is obtained by the licensee, then the licensee must use only original music that the licensee owns and controls. Licensees are solely responsible and liable for all music clearances and shall indemnify the copyright owners of the play(s) and their licensing agent, Samuel French, against any costs, expenses, losses and liabilities arising from the use of music by licensees. Please contact the appropriate music licensing authority in your territory for the rights to any incidental music.

RENTAL MATERIALS

An **Adapter's Guide** and **Piano/Vocal books** will be loaned prior to the production ONLY on the receipt of the Licensing Fee quoted for all performances, the rental fee and a refundable deposit. Please contact Samuel French for perusal of the music materials as well as a performance license application.

TREY PARKER'S CANNIBAL! THE MUSICAL merchandise T-shirts may be purchased at www.totallysweet.net.

IMPORTANT BILLING AND CREDIT REQUIREMENTS

If you have obtained performance rights to this title, please refer to your licensing agreement for important billing and credit requirements.

A NOTE FROM THE AUTHOR

Film is a visual medium. It emphasizes images. There are a lot of cinematic elements in *Cannibal!* which can't be re-created on a stage. Subtitles with city name and year? Panoramic view of The Grand Canyon? How do you do that on stage?

You don't.

When adapting *Cannibal!*, surrender to the limitations of the theater. Keep in mind that plays are verbal. They emphasize language and characters. As you adapt *Cannibal!* for the stage, let go of any attempt to merely re-create the movie on stage. Focus instead on the words. *Cannibal!* contains brilliant dialogue and songs. Imagine the dialogue being spoken in your theater. Visualize where your actors might walk and climb and sing. Let go of any urge to imitate film, and come up with ways to stage the words and songs that fit your space and your budget. There is no wrong way to adapt *Cannibal!*, so long as you maintain the fun of the film.

To get you started, we've created an Acting Edition out of the original screenplay. It contains the dialogue, the song lyrics, and very little else. Minimal stage directions and scene breaks indicate where the characters are and when they might enter and exit a scene. Beyond that, there is no indication how you should stage the scene or what kind of set (if any) you should use. Even the stage directions are suggestions only. You are free to tailor the show to your needs.

CHARACTERS

ALFRED PACKER

SHANNON WILSON BELL

FRANK MILLER

JAMES HUMPHREY

ISRAEL SWAN

GEORGE NOON

FRENCHY CABAZON

O.D. LOUTZENHEISER – Also plays one of the **DADS**, an **UTE INDIAN**, **JUDGE**, and **CYCLOPS**

PRESTON NUTTER – Also plays **MR. MILLS**, one of the **DADS**, both of the **SHERIFFS**

POLLY PRY

LIANNE

CHIEF – Also plays **CYCLOPS**, **GENERAL STORE OWNE**, one of the **DADS**

SETTING

The unsettled territory of Colorado

TIME

19th Century

(**PACKER** *kills the miners one by one.*)

(**PACKER** *rips* **MILLER**'*s jaw from his face, pulls out his tongue, and lifts it over his head ready to eat it like a long piece of spaghetti.*)

(*Crossfade to* **MILLS** *holding up a red handkerchief in the exact same pose as* **PACKER**.)

MILLS. (*screams*) Ahhhhh! And then he cuts up the bodies.

TOWNSFOLK. Oh, gross!

MILLS. And when he finally arrives, tired and beat, he says, "Oh, I don't know what happened to my companions. They left me behind." And everybody believes him. They feel sorry for him, and they just let him go on to Saguache. Now, what would he have you believe? That under these horrible conditions it was justified? No, gentlemen of the jury. It is never justified to murder. Murder is wrong. So I ask you to come back with a verdict to hang this bastard for what he has done. The prosecution rests.

CROWD. Hurray!

PACKER. But that's not the way it happened.

[MUSIC NO. 01: "OVERTURE"]

(*SIGN: "Lake City, Colorado 1883"*)

MILLS. Miss Pry. Hello

POLLY. Oh, hello, Mr. Mills.

MILLS. Busy?

POLLY. I was going to try to get an interview with Mr. Packer.

MILLS. Now, why would you possibly want to spend your afternoon with a beast like that when you could spend it with a gentleman like myself? Huh?

POLLY. Believe me, I don't relish the thought of speaking to him, or even be in the same room with him. But it's what I must do. I am a reporter.

MILLS. Yes, and a most beautiful one at that. Can we meet for dinner, then?

POLLY. Uh…when I'm done here, I'll be at the hotel.

MILLS. At the hotel.

POLLY. If I can get him talking soon enough.

MILLS. I'll give you a hint. If you want to get him talking, ask him about Liane.

POLLY. Liane?

MILLS. Trust me.

(She enters the jail cell.)

POLLY. Hello?

PACKER. The sheriff's gone.

POLLY. Good enough. I'm here to see you, anyway. My name is Polly Pry. I was wondering if I could ask you a few questions about your story.

PACKER. My lawyer says I can't talk to reporters.

POLLY. Yes, of course he did. That's very smart of him. But I'm not a reporter. You see, I'm just a… Well… The truth is, I saw you in the courtroom. And I thought to myself, "How could this handsome, intelligent man have ever done what they say he did."

PACKER. I didn't!

POLLY. And then I thought about how lonely you must be in this dark, nasty cell, all cooped up…

PACKER. Gee, you really think so? This is the nicest place I've lived in a while.

POLLY. …with no one to talk to at all. And then I realized how badly you must need someone to just listen.

PACKER. I do?

POLLY. Uh-huh. And then I thought maybe I should come down here and give you some company. And maybe tell you some secrets. And you can tell me some secrets.

PACKER. Okay.

POLLY. So… What exactly happened during your trip to Breckenridge?

PACKER. I can't talk about that.

POLLY. *(pause)* Okay. Let's talk about something else.

PACKER. Okay.

POLLY. Oh, I know. Why don't you tell me about… *(pause)* …Liane.

PACKER. You know her!?

POLLY. Yes… Yes. I know her well. I wanted to find out a little more about you two. Was she with you on your trip?

PACKER. I don't know. My lawyer's supposed to come back any minute and he gets very angry if…

POLLY. Certainly your lawyer wouldn't mind you talking just a little bit about Liane, especially with someone who's just a simple townsfolk.

PACKER. No, I guess he wouldn't

POLLY. So, what was she like?

PACKER. She was beautiful. She had long, dark, shiny hair, and almond eyes, and little, pointy ears, and a big fluffy tail, and she was fast. Like this. Whoosh!

*(**LIANE** enters.)*

("Bingham Mine, Utah 1873")

PACKER. Come on, girl!

[MUSIC NO. 02: "SHPADOINKLE DAY"]

PACKER.

THE SKY IS BLUE AND ALL THE LEAVES ARE GREEN
THE SUN'S AS WARM AS A BAKED POTATO
I'M SURE YOU KNOW EXACTLY WHAT I MEAN
WHEN I SAY IT'S A SHPADOINKLE DAY

AND AS I RIDE WITH MY GIRL
SHE'S MY BEST FRIEND IN THE WHOLE WORLD
WE MOVE ALONG

SET OUR GOALS HIGH
WITH EYES FULL OF HOPE AS WE AIM FOR THE –

– SKY IS BLUE AND ALL THE LEAVES ARE GREEN
MY HEART'S AS FULL AS A BAKED POTATO
I THINK I KNOW PRECISELY WHAT I MEAN
WHEN I SAY IT'S A SHPADOINKLE DAY

WHEN I SAY IT'S A HAPPY-GO-MOINKEL-Y
LUCKY SHPADOINKLE-Y DAYYYYYY

SWAN. Hey! Mornin', Alf.

PACKER. Mornin', Swan. Find any gold yet?

SWAN. Not in this gosh-darned canyon. That's why a group of us are going to Breckenridge today.

PACKER. Breckenridge? In Colorado Territory?

SWAN. That's the place. Say, you oughta come with us. The more the merrier.

PACKER. Shucks. I'd love to go back to Colorado Territory.

SWAN. I didn't know you were from Colorado Territory.

PACKER. Yeah, I worked in Georgetown for a while before I came here.

SWAN. Huh.

PACKER. Say, who's guiding you there?

SWAN. Lucky Larry. He's from Denver.

PACKER. You think I could talk with Lucky Larry?

SWAN. Sure. I'm going to meet a group of them now.

PACKER. Swell.

*(The miners enter as **BELL** preaches his sermon.)*

BELL. Some have said that Breckenridge is heaven upon this Earth. Let's not forget the story from The Book of Mormon, when Brigham Young planted many corn crops of corn and a band of locusts came and they began to eat his crops. Then the Lord sent down a flock of seagulls and they began to eat the locusts 15 at a time…*(continues in this fashion under the dialogue)*

SWAN. My goodness, what is that?

MINER. That's Lucky Larry. He was struck by lightening last night.

PACKER. Gosh. Is he going to be okay? *(pause)* What?

BELL. We can't let ourselves get discouraged. They say there's enough gold in Breckenridge to build walls out of. The Lord works in mysterious ways and I think this is a test of our will. My fellow Mormons know what I'm talking about. Trials and tribulations. That's what life's all about. Now, are we gonna let this one little thing keep us from fulfilling our dreams?!?

EVERYONE. YES!

BELL. Oh, come on, now. We've got to be strong, don't we?!?

EVERYONE. NO!

BELL. But I'm telling you we can still make it.

MILLER. Our guide is dead!

BELL. There's got to be someone from around here who knows that territory a bit. Anybody?

SWAN. Hey, didn't you say you were from Colorado Territory?

PACKER. Well, I just worked for a little while in –

SWAN. Hey, this guy's from Colorado Territory.

BELL. Wonderful! What's your name, sir?

PACKER. Uh, I'm Alferd Packer. This is my horse, Liane.

(**LIANE** *farts loudly.*)

PACKER. Hi.

BELL. There. You see?

MILLER. Don't be stupid. Let's just go back to mining here.

BELL. But there's no gold here. When's the last time anyone made a strike?

NOON. I'll go.

NOON'S DAD. Now, come on, Son. We'll head out in the spring.

NOON. But Dad, if we wait till the Spring, all the gold'll be gone. I need to go out now.

NOON'S DAD. No! It's too dangerous. What if you get lost, or run out of food?

NOON. Dad, I can't be your little boy forever. Don't you understand?

NOON'S DAD. No, I don't understand. Aw, go ahead. Break your mother's heart.

NOON. I'm in.

BELL. There. You see? Don't you all feel a little bit ashamed? This nice, young, brave…

MILLER. Stupid…

(*The crowd laughs.*)

BELL. Go on and laugh. The lord works in mysterious ways. (*continues under dialogue*)

H'S DAD. Son, why don't you go?

HUMPHERY. Huh?

H'S DAD. You always said you wanted to get out of Utah.

HUMPHERY. No, I didn't.

H'S DAD. Yes you did. I distinctly remember you saying you wanted to get out of Utah and go East.

HUMPHERY. No I didn't!

H'S DAD. Son, don't argue with me. You go to Breckenridge now. You can stake a claim. Me and your brother can come out in the spring.

HUMPHERY. But –

H'S DAD. Son, don't argue with me. (*to* **BELL**) He's in.

(**HUMPHERY**'s *stupid brother giggles.* **HUMPHERY** *smacks him.*)

BELL. Wonderful. That makes five.

MILLER. Good luck. You'll need it.

BELL. That's all.

NOON. Say, when do we leave?

SWAN. The sooner the better, I'd say.

BELL. Well, let's ask our new guide. Mr. Packer?

PACKER. Guess I'm ready whenever you guys are.

BELL. Well, then let's get packin'.

PACKER. What?

[MUSIC NO. 03: "SHPADOINKLE DAY REPRISE"]

BELL.

> IT'S A LONG, LONG WAY FOR US TO GO
> BUT IF WE DON'T TRY, WE'LL NEVER KNOW
> STAY OPTIMISTIC, SET OUR GOALS HIGH
> THERE'S NOTHING WE CAN'T DO IF WE AIM FOR THE—

ALL.

> —SKY IS BLUE AND ALL THE LEAVES ARE GREEN
> THE AIR'S A PURE AS A BAKED POTATO
> WE'RE SURE YOU KNOW EXACTLY WHAT WE MEAN
> WHEN WE SAY IT'S A SHPADOINKLE DAY
>
> WHEN WE SAY IT'S A SHPADOINKLE DAY

MILLER. Hey! How long's it gonna take?

PACKER. Oh, not more than, like, three weeks at the most.

MILLER. All right. Let's go.

[MUSIC NO. 04: "DON'T BE STUPID"]

TOWNSPEOPLE:

> DON'T BE STUPID
> WAIT UNTIL SPRING
> THE MOUNTAINS IN THE WINTER ARE
> A TREACHEROUS THING
> JUST LOOK AT THESE FOOLS
> THEY THINK THEY CAN MAKE IT
> IT'LL BE TWENTY BELOW
> AND THEY SAY THEY CAN TAKE IT
> WHAT A BUNCH OF STUPID MOTHER-F –

*(Everyone except **PACKER** exits.)*

(INSERT: map)

PACKER. So Liane and I headed east with the other miners, thinking it would be a nice, happy trip. But then four weeks later, we were just outside of Provo.

(The miners re-enter.)

MILLER. Three weeks my ass, Packer.

PACKER. That's when I got my first bad feeling.

NOON. Jeez. It sure is a lot of walking. I swear, my legs are killing me. How much further to Provo?

PACKER. We've got to be really close now.

BELL. And then from Provo, how far is it to Breckenridge?

PACKER. See, I always have Liane with me when I come out, so I don't know how long it's gonna take us on foot.

HUMPHERY. Gosh, I sure wish I had a horse. How much did you pay for yours, Packer?

PACKER. I didn't. She's been mine since I was little.

SWAN. Well she certainly is a shpadoinkle horse.

(The **DOOMED GUY** *enters.)*

PACKER. Oh, hello. Could you tell us how much further it is to Provo?

BELL. We have to get some supplies for our big trip into the Rocky Mountains.

DOOMED GUY. You'll never come back again. It's got a curse on it.

HUMPHERY. Provo?

DOOMED GUY. The Rocky Mountains. I gotta warn you. You're doomed! Doomed! Doomed! You're doomed! Doomed! Turn back while you still can. You're doomed. You're all doomed! *(exits)*

PACKER AND BELL. Thank you.

*(***THE MINERS*** enter a general store. The* **OWNER** *is behind the counter.* **PACKER** *ties* **LIANE** *to a hitching post in front of the store.)*

BELL. Howdy.

CLERK. Howdy.

SWAN: Howdy.

CLERK. Howdy.

NOON. Howdy-do?

CLERK. Howdy.

HUMPHERY. Howdy.

CLERK. Howdy-do.

MILLER. Howdy.

CLERK. Howdy.

PACKER. Howdy-do.

CLERK. Howdy.

PACKER. Hey, they've got maps of Colorado Territory.

MILLER. Jesus! Now he needs a fucking map!

BELL. Miller, if you don't want to go, then don't go. But if you can't get along with the others, I'm gonna have to put you in Time Out.

MILLER. In what?

BELL. Anyone who can't get along with the others has to sit 20 feet away, by themselves, for an hour.

SWAN. That's a good idea. It gives you a chance to cool down when things get steamed up.

BELL. Exactly.

MILLER. You've gotta be kidding me.

HUMPHERY. You guys! They have fudge here!

NOON. What about blankets? Shouldn't we get more?

BELL. That's a good idea. Let's just do this as quickly as possible. I think we're already running a little behind schedule.

MILLER. What schedule!?

(**THE TRAPPERS** *enter. They fawn over* **LIANE**. **PACKER** *sees this and runs out of the store.*)

SWAN. Do we have a schedule, Mr. Packer? Mr. Packer?

FRENCHY. This your horse?

PACKER. Yup.

FRENCHY. Purty.

PACKER. I'm Alferd Packer.

FRENCHY. Frenchy Cabazon.

PACKER. Oh, you're French.

FRENCHY. No.

PACKER. Oh.

FRENCHY. We're just stopping through your quaint little town here on the way to Colorado Territory.

PACKER. Oh, I'm not from here. In fact, I'm leading a party to Colorado Territory myself.

NUTTER. Whereabouts?

PACKER. Breckenridge.

FRENCHY. Is that near Saguache?

PACKER. Saguache is… Uh, yeah. Yeah. It's near Saguache.

FRENCHY. Say, you gents wanna trade some furs for the trip? We got rabbits and beavers.

SWAN. Ugh! How horrible.

HUMPHERY. Oh, where'd you guys get all those little dead animals?

LOUTZENHEIZER. We're trappers, stupid.

PACKER. Poor little bunny rabbits.

FRENCHY. I figured you were all trappers, too. She's an Arabian, ain't she?

PACKER. Yeah.

FRENCHY. Arabian's a trapper horse.

LOUTZENHEIZER. You ain't trappers.

MILLER. No, we're miners.

NUTTER. You're diggers!

LOUTZENHEIZER. Trapper horse ain't supposed to be with no digger.

HUMPHERY. Nice hat.

FRENCHY. Oh, boy! A bunch of diggers traipsing around the Rockies in the middle of winter. That's rich!

NUTTER. I'll say.

FRENCHY. Don't you boys know how scary the mountains are? What are you gonna do if you run into some Injuns? Or the Cyclops?

HUMPHERY. There's no Cyclops in the Rocky Mountains. Is there, you guys?

BELL. We're not afraid of anything. We have Jesus on our side.

FRENCHY. Oh, well, if you're not scared of anything.

(**FRENCHY** *suddenly turns on* **PACKER** *and screams at him.* **PACKER** *falls to the ground.*)

FRENCHY. Have a nice trip, boys.

BELL. Good bye!

SWAN. So, who's cooking dinner tonight?

HUMPHERY. I'll cook. I'm a great cook.

MILLER. Humphrey, everyone knows you're a chronic liar.

HUMPHERY. But I can! I'm a super cook!

(*The miners set up camp.* **HUMPHREY** *cooks some gross mushy stuff.*)

MILLER. You son of a bitch, Humphery.

HUMPHERY. Aw, come on. You haven't even tried it yet.

MILLER. You son of a bitch, Humphery.

SWAN. Mmmmmm! This stuff is great! Could I have more of the yellow stuff?

PACKER. Hey, do you guys think it's true, that she's a trapper horse?

BELL. Oh, a horse is a horse.

HUMPHERY. Of course.

PACKER. Of course. But I don't think Arabians even are trapper horses, are they?

SWAN. What matters, Mr. Packer, is that you're good to that horse. Trappers never are.

BELL. He's right.

MILLER. God, you guys make me sick. What is this, a feel-good convention?

BELL. Now listen. We've got a long journey ahead of us. It's important that we all get along. Now, you're hurting people's feelings. You're going to have to find a more constructive way to express your anger.

MILLER. Okay. Well, fuck you. How's that for constructive?

BELL. That's great. Now go to Time Out, mister.

SWAN. We warned you.

MILLER. God, you guys are weird.

BELL. Ah-ah-ah! Twenty feet away. Turn around. You know the rules.

NOON. Man, I just can't wait to get to Breckenridge and see all those pretty women.

SWAN. That's really all you care about, isn't it, Mr. Noon?

NOON. I've been hiking around with my dad mining for ages. I mean, it's like the only people we ever see are guys. I think the only time I've ever seen women is in Salt Lake City. And the women there are just so…

HUMPHERY. Mormon.

NOON. I mean, I'm 19 now. You know? I just want to get in there and see what it feels like to… You know.

PACKER. What?

BELL. Well, young man, if there's half as much gold in those hills as people say, you'll be rich. And you won't have to worry about…that.

PACKER. What? What?

[MUSIC NO. 05: "THAT'S ALL I'M ASKING FOR"]

NOON.

(spoken)

I know that there's more to life than women.

I just can't seem to figure out what else there is.

I don't need it every night.

Every morning would be just fine.

A little sex – That's all I'm asking for.

(sings)

THAT'S ALL I'M ASKING FOR

BELL AND SWAN.

THAT'S ALL HE'S ASKING FOR

NOON.

SOMETHING I CAN TEST

A GAL WOULD SUIT ME BEST
I GOT A THING TO USE
I KNOW WHAT TO USE IT FOR
A GIRL I CAN LOVE AND KISS AND HOLD AND FU—
THAT'S ALL I'M ASKING FOR

BELL.

NOW I DON'T WANT TO BE RICH FOR THE SAKE OF WOMEN
I WANT TO BE RICH FOR THE SAKE OF OUR LORD
ENOUGH TO BUILD A CHURCH
WHERE EVERYONE CAN COME
ENOUGH FOR THE LORD – THAT'S ALL I'M ASKING FOR
THAT'S ALL I'M ASKING FOR

PACKER AND SWAN.

THAT'S ALL HE'S ASKING FOR

HUMPHERY.

IT AIN'T A LOT TO ASK
I'M SURE WE'LL GET IT FAST
A FRIEND OF MINE WAS MINING
AND HE MADE A LOT OF CASH
HE MADE A GAZILLION DOLLARS
HOW IS THAT? – THAT'S ALL I'M ASKING FOR

MILLER. *(spoken)* He did not make a gazillion dollars.

HUMPHERY. You wanna ask him? I'll tell you where he lives.

NOON AND BELL AND PACKER.

(singing)

THAT'S ALL HE'S ASKING FOR

HUMPHERY.

THAT'S ALL I'M ASKING FOR

SWAN.

WE'RE TIRED OF BEING SICK
WE'RE SICK OF BEING POOR
WE'VE HAD A LITTLE LUCK NOW WE WANT A LITTLE MORE

SWAN, BELL, NOON AND HUMPHERY.

ENOUGH SO WE'D NEVER DO ANYTHING ANYMORE
THAT'S ALL WE'RE ASKING FOR

SWAN. *(spoken)* Hey, what about you, Mr. Miller? What are you asking for?

MILLER. No. No. I don't sing.

BELL. Aw, come on. If you can talk, you can sing.

MILLER. I just want to make enough so I can open up a shop of my own and go on with my family trade.

BELL. Well, there. That's great. What is it you do?

MILLER. I'm a butcher.

NOON. You're a butcher?

MILLER. Yeah.

PACKER.

I'VE NEVER HAD MUCH IN THE WAY OF FRIENDS OR FAMILY
MY HORSE IS THE ONLY PAL I'VE EVER KNOWN
I'D LIKE TO BUILD A RANCH IN THE ROCKY MOUNTAIN AIR
A HOME FOR US – THAT'S ALL I'M ASKING FOR

PACKER, NOON, SWAN, BELL, HUMPHERY:
THAT'S ALL WE'RE ASKING FOR
THAT'S ALL WE'RE ASKING FOR
WE'RE TIRED OF BEING SICK
WE'RE SICK OF BEING POOR
WE'VE HAD A LITTLE LUCK
NOW WE WANT A LITTLE MORE

NOON. A girl I can love!

BELL. A church!

PACKER. A ranch!

MILLER. *(spoken)* A store.

PACKER, NOON, SWAN, BELL, HUMPHERY:
THAT'S ALL WE'RE ASKING–
THAT'S ALL WE'RE ASKING–
THAT'S ALL WE'RE ASKING FOR!

PACKER. You know, the thing I think I want more than anything is just to go south to Saguache and find those trappers and walk right up to them and go, "Ha! We made it."

DOOMED GUY. *(offstage)* You're doomed! You're all doomed.

(Lights out)

(The next morning:)

PACKER. Liane! Liane! I don't know where she could've gone.

NOON. You had her tied up, didn't you?

PACKER. No, I never do. Liane!

HUMPHERY. This is my house.

BELL. What's going on here?

NOON. Packer's horse left.

MILLER. What? Our food was on that horse!

HUMPHERY. Shut up, you guys. I'm tired!

PACKER. She'll be back. She probably just went on ahead to find some water or something. Liane! HERE, GIRL!

BELL. Hey, come on, Packer. We should get going.

PACKER. What? No. I can't go now. I've got to find her.

MILLER. Whoa, whoa whoa! Look, asshole. You said you'd take us to Breckenridge. You're not going to leave us here to find it ourselves.

PACKER. I'm not going to leave here without her.

MILLER. I say you are.

BELL. We've got to keep moving, Packer, especially now that we've lost all our food. We've got to get to the next town as soon as possible.

NOON. Hey, Packer. It looks like her trails lead off that way. Maybe she's in front of us.

PACKER. Okay.

*(All of the miners exit except for **PACKER**.)*

PACKER. *(from jail cell)* Liane's tracks headed east, so I kept following them. The men didn't care as long as we were aiming for Breckenridge. And then something happened that changed everything.

*(**THE MINERS** re-enter.)*

PACKER. HERE, GIRL!

HUMPHERY. How far to Colorado Territory?

PACKER. I don't know. We must be pretty close. Liane! HERE, GIRL! She's lost.

MILLER. She's not lost. She just took off.

PACKER. No, she didn't just take off. We were friends, and friends don't just take off.

HUMPHERY. Watch out for that bear trap.

BELL. What? *(steps in bear trap)* AHHHHH!!!!! SHPADOINKLE!!! AHHHHHH!!! *(continues to ad lib screams of pain and anger)*

MILLER. Get it open!

HUMPHERY. No, you're doing it wrong. you have to do it like this…

BELL. Ahhhhh.

HUMPHREY. Woops:

BELL. Ahhhhh.

PACKER. Let me try. You okay?

BELL. Who the heck put a trap here?!?

MILLER. It's not that bad, is it?

BELL. I don't know. Let me see.

(**BELL** *kicks* **HUMPHREY** *in the ass.*)

HUMPHERY. Ow.

BELL. Yeah, it's fine.

HUMPHERY. Hey, look, you guys! The Green River!

(The Green River flows onstage.)

BELL. Boy, I'm not having much luck on this trip, am I?

SWAN. Look on the bright side. At least you didn't get your head caught in that thing.

NOON. How the hell are we supposed to cross this?

PACKER. Wait. There's supposed to be a bridge. We must be too far north. Or too far south.

MILLER. Some guide!

HUMPHERY. Okay. We can take our wheelbarrow, build it into a little boat, and then ride it across, and then build it back into a wheelbarrow again.

NOON. Talk about a wasting time. Don't be such a horse's ass. *(PACKER reacts.)* Sorry, Packer. How deep do you think it is?

(PACKER throws a rock into the river.)

MILLER. What the HELL was that supposed to prove?

PACKER. Well… It… I don't know.

BELL. Let's just see what we can carry.

NOON. You really think we can make it?

SWAN. Sure, as long as we all go at once. That way, if one of us trips and starts shooting downstream, we'll all be there to catch him.

NOON. Downstream?

MILLER. Nobody's going downstream.

HUMPHERY. This is gonna suck.

BELL. Okay… On "three." One… Two…

(SWAN jumps in.)

BELL. THREE!

(The miners get swept down stream and eventually cross the river.)

NOON. My balls! Oh, my god! I can't feel my balls.

PACKER. Wait. I think we lost Humphery.

MILLER. Good!

BELL. Hey, Packer. Are there any more big rivers between here and Breckenridge?

PACKER. No, just the Colorado.

NOON. You guys, I can't feel my balls!!!

SWAN. We better set up and camp quick and get out of these clothes or else we're gonna get hypothermia something awful.

BELL. He's right. We've gotta get some body heat going.

(**THE MINERS** *set up camp and climb into sleeping bags.*)

NOON. Yeah. I'm starting to feel them again. Whew! That scared the shit out of me.

HUMPHERY. Gosh, I never thought I'd be sleeping next to a naked man on this trip.

NOON. Just do what I'm doing. Just pretend like you're laying next to a nice soft woman.

MILLER. What?!?

NOON. I'm just imagining old Mr. Miller here as a nice, tall blond with…

MILLER. Aw, goddammit. I want a different partner.

BELL. You know, I think we should all take a minute and thank the Lord for getting us across that river.

ALL. (*mumble mumble mumble*) Amen.

HUMPHERY. I can't go on. I'm so hungry. Oh, wait! I've got some fudge.

NOON. Say, Packer. You really miss Liane, don't you?

PACKER. Boy, I'll say. I just can't believe she'd just take off like that.

SWAN. Don't worry, Mr. Packer. There's plenty of horses in the world. You'll find another one.

PACKER. Wouldn't want another one.

[MUSIC NO. 06: "WHEN I WAS ON TOP OF YOU"]

PACKER.

SHE'LL NEVER KNOW
WHAT SHE MEANT TO ME
WHENEVER I WAS WITH HER
I WAS ALWAYS AS GENTLE AS I COULD BE
AND NOW I DON'T KNOW WHY, BUT SHE'S GONE AWAY
AND I'LL JUST HAVE TO STAND ON MY OWN TWO LEGS

YOUR EYES, YOUR SMILE
MADE MY LITTLE LIFE WORTHWHILE
THERE WAS NOTHING I COULDN'T DO
WHEN I WAS ON TOP OF YOU

I'D PULL HER HAIR
SHE'D KNOW TO STOP
AND WHEN SHE LOOKED BEHIND HER
I'D ALWAYS BE THERE
AND NOW I DON'T KNOW WHY BUT, SHE... SHE'S GONE
AND ALL I CAN DO IS TRY TO CARRY ON

YOUR EYES, YOUR SMILE
MADE MY LITTLE LIFE WORTHWHILE
THE SKY WAS A LOT MORE BLUE
WHEN I WAS ON TOP OF YOU

WHEN I WAS ON TOP OF YOU

HUMPHERY. Fudge, Packer?

(**THE MINERS** *go to sleep.*)

(**PACKER** *returns to his cell; the miners exit.*)

PACKER. She was the only thing I ever had. The only thing that made me feel important. The only thing that made me feel wanted. That night, I swore I'd get those men to Breckenridge as fast as I possibly could, and then go back and find her.

POLLY. So, that was the last time you ever saw her.

PACKER. No, I saw her again, all right.

POLLY. The trappers took her?

PACKER. I don't know if anybody took her, but then a few weeks later, we crossed over into Colorado Territory.

(**THE MINERS** *enter, soaking wet.*)

HUMPHERY. "Are there any more big rivers between here and Breckenridge?" "Oh, no, just the Colorado." The biggest FUCKING river I've seen in my entire life thank you very much, he said dripping with water.

PACKER. It didn't used to be that big.

BELL. I suppose we should all get into our bags again and –

MILLER. NO! NO! NO! Let's just keep walking, at least until the sun goes down. It ain't that cold.

(**THE MINERS** *come to the edge of the Grand Canyon.*)

MILLER. Oh, this is good, Packer. Real good. You're just a regular Christopher Columbus, aren't you?

PACKER. We made it. This is Colorado Territory.

NOON. Looks like we're gonna make it after all.

PACKER. Come on. We can just walk around it. It can't be that big.

SWAN. Hey, look you guys! Snow!

(**SWAN** *runs offstage.*)

(*The* **UTES** *enter.*)

BELL. What is it, Packer?

PACKER. Up over that ridge.

MILLER. Utes.

PACKER. No, I think they're Indians.

BELL. Utes are Indians.

(**SWAN** *pokes his head onstage.*)

SWAN. Hey, you guys wanna build a snowman or something?

BELL. Shut up, Swan! Come on. Let's get down.

(**THE MINERS** *lie down in plain sight and put their hands over their eyes.*)

PACKER. You think they see us?

BELL. I don't know.

UTE 1. Nanimonoda? (*"Who are you?"*)

BELL. Mornin'.

PACKER. Mornin'.

BELL. Oh, shit.

UTE 2. Kitanai minari shiy agatte. (*"You are wearing fucking dirty clothes."*)

(*The* **UTES** *laugh at their private joke. The miners laugh nervously and have no idea what the* **UTES** *are saying.*)

BELL. What is that? Ute?

PACKER. I don't know.

UTE 1. Momotaro mitaidana. (*"You look like Momotaro"* [*a character in a Japanese children's story*])

NOON. What the hell kinda language is that?

PACKER. I don't know. Just keep laughing.

HUMPHERY. Wait, you guys. Lemme talk to them. I know how to speak Indian.

BELL. We're gonna die.

HUMPHERY. Weep wah, weep wah, surrow noh happo.

UTE 2. Nani ittenno? (*"What did you say?"*)

HUMPHERY. Hmmm. He says, "Welcome to the land of blue light."

UTE 2. Sakanato issyoni nemurasete yaruzo! (*"Keep it up and you'll be sleeping with the fishes, see?!"*)

HUMPHERY. "I am a carpenter, and this is my brother, Tom."

MILLER. Humphery, you are so full of shit!

PACKER. Ask them if they've seen a brown horse with a freckled nose.

BELL. He doesn't know what they're saying.

(*A snowball come flying from offstage and hits* **BELL** *in the head.* **SWAN** *enters, laughing.*)

SWAN. Ha ha ha ha ha. Gotcha!

(**MILLER** *uses the distraction to pull his gun on the* **UTES**. *The* **UTES** *karate-chop the gun out of* **MILLER** *'s hand, then swiftly point their swords at* **HUMPHREY** *'s throat.*)

UTE 1. Nanda?! Sugu kotchi koi!! Haiyaku! Haiyaku! (*"What the heck?! Come here immediately!! Quickly! Quickly!"*)

UTE 2. Kuso, bakayaro! Konna shibaiwa daikiraida! (*"Fuck you! I really hate this play!"*)

HUMPHERY. Uh, you guys, I think they want us to follow them.

UTE 1. Ike! Korette sugoi bakana shibaidana! (*"Go ahead! This is a really stupid play."*)

PACKER. What should we do?

NOON. Maybe they just want Humphery.

UTE 1. Kocchi koi! (*"Come on!"*)

BELL. Guess we don't have much choice.

NOON. We're in a lot of trouble here, aren't we?

BELL. Just stay calm. Let me do the talking. Humphery, don't say anything.

> (*The* **UTES** *lead* **THE MINERS** *offstage.*)

> (*The* **CHIEF** *enters with his teepees.*)

> (*The* **UTES** *enter with* **THE MINERS**.)

MILLER. This is the weirdest Indian tribe I've ever seen.

CHIEF. Ya! Ya! Ya! Yoku kita na! Kimi ga kono eiga no shujinkoo na n daroo? (Hi! Hi! Hi! Welcome! I guess you are the hero of this movie?)

HUMPHERY. He says…

CHIEF. Who are you assholes?

HUMPHERY. Oh, he speaks English.

> (**UTE 1** *speaks Japanese to* **CHIEF**.)

BELL. We are from Utah. Uuuuu-tahhhhh.

CHIEF. Ah! Utah! Ah!

BELL. Could you tell me what tribe this is?

CHIEF. We are Indians.

BELL. Yes, I see that, but what Indians?

CHIEF. You don't think we are Indians?

BELL. No, no, I just….

CHIEF. We have tee-pees.

BELL. Right. I see. But…

CHIEF. Look at all these tee-pees we have. Because we are Indians.

PACKER. Yeah, they have tee-pees.

CHIEF. Where is your destination?

PACKER. Breckenridge.

BELL. It's a small town east of here.

CHIEF. I know. There are lots of gold there.

SWAN. Yeah, that's the place!

(*A cute* SQUAW *enters.* NOON*'s hormones soar.*)

CHIEF. I'm afraid there is terrible storm in the mountain. So if you like, you may wait here with us and other assholes for storm to calm down.

PACKER. What other assholes?

CHIEF. Ten days ago, a group of assholes like yourselves came through here. I told them they should wait for the storm to end.

BELL. Where are they?

CHIEF. Junichi will take you to them. But don't take too long, because dinner in one hour.

BELL. Thank you… Chief.

(*The* CHIEF *and all of the miners except* NOON *exit.*)

NOON. (*to* SQUAW) Yep yep yep yep yep. I like your feather. Yep yep yep yep yep.

(NOON *and the* SQUAW *exit.*)

(THE MINERS *re-enter.*)

MILLER. Hey, screw this, man. If they're not keeping us here, let's just ask for some food and be on our way.

HUMPHERY. Yeah. We wanna get to Breckenridge before all the gold's worked out. Remember?

BELL. I don't know. I really think we ought to wait that storm out.

NOON. Yeah. Me, too.

SWAN. Indians know what they're talking about when it comes to weather.

(THE TRAPPERS *enter.*)

FRENCHY. Well, lookie who's here!

PACKER. Oh, crap.

FRENCHY. So, you guys were lucky enough to run into the Nihonjin too, eh? Good thing. You diggers would've died for sure in that storm. Say, what happened to your horse, Packer?

HUMPHERY. She ran away. What?

FRENCHY. Boy, that's a stitch.

NUTTER. I'll say.

PACKER. What's so funny?

FRENCHY. Come on, Packer. It was only a matter of time. A trapper horse can't spend her whole life with no boring, dumb, Cheezmo miner.

PACKER. Well, it's better than just leaving traps where people can step in 'em and stuff.

NOON. Yeah, and killing all those furry little animals all the time.

LOUTZENHEIZER. Awwww. Don't hurt the wittle animals.

HUMPHERY. Nice hat!

PACKER. I'd rather be a miner than a trapper any day.

FRENCHY. You guys don't know what it means to be a trapper!

NUTTER. Yeah! Tell 'em, French.

[MUSIC NO. 07: "THE TRAPPER SONG"]

FRENCHY.

> I CAN CATCH A HELPLESS ANIMAL
> SKIN IT WITH MY BARE HANDS
> I WAKE UP MUDDY
> AND I GO TO BED BLOODY
> CUZ I'M A TRAPPIN' MAN
>
> I CAN BRAVE THE NASTIEST WEATHER

LOUTZENHEIZER & NUTTER: *(spoken)* Weather!

FRENCHY.

> EVEN IF IT'S 80 BELOW

LOUTZENHEIZER & NUTTER. *(spoken)* Below!

FRENCHY.

> MY PA WAS AN ELEPHANT
> BUT THAT'S IRRELEVANT
> MY MA WAS AN ESKIMO

I EAT RABBITS' HEADS FOR BREAKFAST

LOUTZENHEIZER & NUTTER. *(spoken)* Breakfast!

FRENCHY.

WITH BEAVER BUTT ON THE SIDE

LOUTZENHEIZER & NUTTER. *(spoken)* The side!

FRENCHY.

MY MIND'S MAGNIFICENT
MY BODY, NO DIFF-ER-ENT
I'M FULL OF TRAPPER PRIDE!

(off-tune) YO-HO!

NUTTER.

(badly off-tune) YO-HO!

LOUTZENHEIZER.

(very badly off-tune) YO-HO!

FRENCHY.

RIP THEIR FUR
CUT THEIR SKIN WITH MY KNIFE
YO-HO!

NUTTER.

YO-HO!

LOUTZENHEIZER.

(badly off-tune) YO-HO!

FRENCHY.

ONE THING'S FOR SURE
NOTHING LIKE THE TRAPPIN' LIFE

I'M BADDER THAN THE BADDEST SAILOR

LOUTZENHEIZER & NUTTER: *(spoken)* Sailor!

FRENCHY.

MAKE LOVE TO WOMEN TEN FEET TALL

LOUTZENHEIZER & NUTTER. *(spoken)* Feet tall!

FRENCHY.

I'VE GOT A CHEST OF WONDER
AND BALLS OF THUNDER

I CAN BREAK RIGHT THROUGH A WALL

I LOVE THE SOUND OF METAL

LOUTZENHEIZER & NUTTER. *(spoken)* Metal!

FRENCHY.

SNAPPING ON AN ANIMAL'S HEAD

LOUTZENHEIZER & NUTTER. *(spoken)* Ka-ching!

FRENCHY.

SOMETIMES THEY SCAMPER
SOMETIMES THEY WIMPER
BUT THEY ALWAYS END UP DEAD

LOUTZENHEIZER.

(sweetly, slowly)

I'VE ALWAYS WANTED TO BE SOMEBODY
WHO DIDN'T GET PUSHED AROUND
NOW THAT I'M A TRAPPER
I'M THE MEANEST GUY AROUND

FRENCHY. *(spoken)* Second-meanest!

THE BLOOD OF A FRESH-CUT RODENT
IS AS SWEET AS BRANDY WINE
AND THE BRAIN OF AN ANTELOPE
TASTES LIKE CANTALOUPE
WHAT A YUMMY LIFE

YO-HO!

NUTTER.

YO-HO!

LOUTZENHEIZER.

(badly off-tune) YO-HO!

FRENCHY.

RIP THEIR FUR
CUT THEIR EYES OUT WITH MY KNIFE

YO-HO!

NUTTER.

YO-HO!

LOUTZENHEIZER:

(badly off-tune) YO-HO!

NOON. Oh, stop!

HUMPHERY. That's sick!

FRENCHY. I agree. Nutter was singing in the wrong key.

NUTTER: No I wasn't. It was Loutzenheizer. I was singing in E-flat minor.

FRENCHY. The song's in F-sharp major!

BELL. I think they're the same thing. I mean, E-flat is the relative minor of F-sharp.

FRENCHY. No it isn't. The relative minor is three half-tones UP from the major, not DOWN!

NOON. No, it's three down. Like A is the relative minor of C-major.

LOUTZENHEIZER. But isn't A-sharp in C-major?

BELL. Wait. Are you singing Mixolydian scales or something?

FRENCHY. A-sharp is tonic to C-major. It's the 6th!

HUMPHERY. No it isn't!

SWAN. It'd be like a raised 13th if anything.

FRENCHY. Oh, well. You guys are just a bunch of loser diggers, anyhow.

HUMPHERY. Oh, see?!? You know we're right!

PACKER. I knew it! This is Liane's food bag. You dirty so-and-so! Where is she?

FRENCHY. I don't know what you're talking about. We found that on the way up here.

PACKER. You're a liar!

FRENCHY. Are you calling me a liar?

PACKER. Yes.

NUTTER. You'd be wise to get out of here, buddy.

PACKER. Look, Frenchy. You know where she is and I'd really like to…

(**FRENCHY** *punches* **PACKER.** *He falls back into* **BELL.** *They both fall to the ground.*)

BELL. Ooof! Ow! That smarts! Ow!

FRENCHY. Nobody, but nobody calls Frenchy Cabazon a liar.

SWAN. Hey, now. Do you need to go to Time Out?

*(**FRENCHY** punches **SWAN**.)*

FRENCHY. Anyone else want to try? Huh? Huh? Now get outta my personal space!

*(**THE MINERS** exit. **PACKER** goes to his jail cell.)*

PACKER. We stayed at the Indian camp and I watched the trappers' every move.

*(The **SHERIFF** of Lake City enters.)*

SHERIFF. Oh, you got him going on about the horse again, did ya? Come on. It's time to go back to the Courthouse.

*(They go to the courtroom. A Townsfolk hits **PACKER** in the back of the head with something. The **JUDGE** and **MILLS** enter.)*

PACKER. Ow.

JUDGE. The defendant will rise. Alferd Packer, a jury of 12 honest citizens have sat in judgment on your case and have found you… GUILTY. Alferd Packer, the judgment of this court is that you be removed from hence to the jail of Hinsdale County and then be taken to a place of execution prepared for this purpose within the limits of the town of Lake City, and then and there be hung by the neck until you are dead… DEAD… DEAD! And may God have mercy on your soul.

*(The **SHERIFF** leads **PACKER** off. **PACKER** stops and listens to the following conversation.)*

MILLS. Hey! We won!

POLLY. Yes, you certainly did.

MILLS. So I don't suppose it will be hard for a winning prosecuting attorney to get a date for dinner?

POLLY. No, I don't suppose it will.

(*The* **SHERIFF** *roughly pulls* **PACKER** *off and puts him back in his cell*)

(**MILLS**, *excited, walks away.*)

POLLY. Asshole.

(*consulting her notes*) "It was then that Packer's horse, his only friend, ran away. Did this loss lead to his murdering and eating his…unsuspecting… companions? What could've caused his madness?"

I can't imagine him being so violent. He seems so harmless. Why should I care?

[MUSIC NO. 08 "THIS SIDE OF ME."]

WHAT IS THIS MAGIC I FEEL
SEEMS NO MATTER WHERE I AM IT FINDS ME
PUTS THE MEMORIES OF HOPE INSIDE ME
MAKES ME WARM ONCE MORE

HE'S JUST A QUIET MAN
BUT HIS EYES CAN SEE RIGHT THROUGH ME
IS IT ONLY THAT I FEEL PITY?
COULD IT BE SOMETHING MORE?

SAFE AS AN ISLAND
FAR OFF TO SEA
I'D ALMOST FORGOTTEN
THIS SIDE OF ME

WHAT IS THIS MAGIC I FEEL
I THOUGHT THIS MUSHY STUFF WAS BELOW ME
COULD IT BE HE IS THE ONE TO SHOW ME
WHAT COMPASSION IS FOR?

SAFE AS AN ISLAND
FAR OFF TO SEA
I'D ALMOST FORGOTTEN
THIS SIDE OF ME

PERHAPS I'M NOT THE COLD BITCH I PRETENDED TO BE
I'D ALMOST FORGOTTEN THIS SIDE OF ME

(**POLLY** *gets an idea. She rushes to* **PACKER**'s *cell.*)

POLLY. Hello, Mr. Packer. How are you doing?

PACKER. How am I doing? Have you ever been sitting around waiting to die?

POLLY. Yes, I have, as a matter of fact.

PACKER. When?

POLLY. Well, all right. I've never, really.

PACKER. Didn't think so.

POLLY. Now, you left the Indian camp January. How long before you realized…

PACKER. Oh, no, no, no, no. What's the point? I told you what I told you because I thought you cared. I didn't realize you were the prosecuting attorney's girl.

POLLY. I am not his girl! I just met the man last week!

PACKER. Great guy.

POLLY. Are you jealous?

PACKER. Why the hell would I be jealous? I'm gonna die tomorrow.

POLLY. He says I shouldn't believe a word you say. He said you went mad at that bar in Saguache.

PACKER. Oh, that's the biggest joke ever. You wanna know what happened? Okay. We were at the Indian camp. It was the morning after another big snow, and it was also the first time I noticed Bell getting edgy.

*(The **UTES** and **CHIEF** enter. They teach **PACKER** some self-defense moves.)*

CHIEF. Your skill is improving, Packer-san.

PACKER. Thanks, Chief. Hey…uh, when do you think I'd be able to use this stuff against, like, two big guys and one short but tough one?

CHIEF. You mean those crazy trappers?

PACKER. Yeah.

CHIEF. Oh, remember, this practice we do is not for becoming bully, okay?

PACKER. Okay.

CHIEF. Besides, you have nothing to worry about. Those crazy trappers left this morning.

PACKER. Oh, really? Good. *(He does a double-take.)* THEY WHAT!?!

CHIEF. Yeah. They decided to go ahead. Although I told them not to. Those crazy trappers.

PACKER. You're kidding!

CHIEF. No, I am not.

PACKER. You're not kidding!

*(**PACKER** runs offstage. The **UTES** follow him, confused.)*

*(The **OTHER MINERS** and **SQUAW** enter.)*

NOON. I may look tough and mean-spirited, but I'm really a sensitive artist.

SQUAW. That's very interesting.

NOON. I paint. And I sculpt. With my hands.

SQUAW. That's very interesting, too.

NOON. You have no idea what I'm saying, do you?

SQUAW. That's very interesting.

*(**PACKER** enters, with the **UTES** and **CHIEF** not too far behind.)*

PACKER. Shpadoinkle! We have to go. I mean, we should be going.

NOON. What?!?

PACKER. The trappers left this morning.

NOON. So?

PACKER. So?!? So…maybe they saw a break in the weather.

NOON. I'm not going anywhere.

PACKER. Come on, you guys. Have you forgotten your dreams? We wanted to get to Breckenridge before all the gold was gone. Remember?

NOON. No way! No way!

BELL. Now, now… Let's think about this. If the trappers saw a break in the storm, that could mean something.

This could be the last chance we get to get out of here for months.

NOON. It's the middle of the winter. You heard the Chief. He said to stay here. Remember? He said…

BELL. Calm down. Calm down. Okay? Breckenridge can't be that far, right?

PACKER. Yeah!

BELL. Besides, if you stopped acting like a *(yells)* SEX-STARVED LITTLE MR. PERVERT, we'd be able to get outta here!!!

SQUAW. Ha-ha-ha-ha-ha! Okay!

CHIEF. What?!? You're leaving? You're crazy, too!

BELL. That gold can't wait for us any longer.

CHIEF. I give you enough food for the trip. Okay?

BELL. Thanks, Chief. Goodbye!

PACKER. See ya, Chief!

SWAN. Shpadoinkle!

(**THE MINERS** *exit;* **PACKER** *goes to his cell)*

CHIEF. Watch out for Cyclops!

(The **UTES** *and* **CHIEF** *exit.)*

PACKER. I may be slow sometimes, but I'm not stupid. I knew the trappers had kidnaped Liane and that she was waiting for me to save her. I thought I could catch up to them on their way to Saguache, but then I got us kinda lost.

(**THE MINERS** *enter.)*

BELL. This doesn't look right, Packer!

PACKER. Chief said to follow the river east. We're following the river east.

BELL. Yeah, but he didn't say anything about this!

NOON. I can't go on anymore. I'm starving.

MILLER. Don't be such a wimp.

(**BELL** *pulls up his pants leg to check his bear trap wound. It is gross and festering and gangrenous)*

HUMPHERY. EWW!

BELL. This trip can't get any worse for me.

SWAN. This canyon is so beautiful!

PACKER. …and so we kept heading for Breckenridge, the snow storms kept getting worse and it wasn't long before we were deep in the Rocky Mountains.

PACKER. We gotta be really close now.

NOON. I can't go on. I need food. I can't…

HUMPHERY. Me, neither. I'm starving.

(*A little sheep enters, looking lost and adorable.*)

PACKER. Look!

HUMPHERY. A sheep!

MILLER. Yes!

(**NOON** *unzips his pants.*)

PACKER. No, no, no. To eat.

NOON. I know. I gotta take a piss.

PACKER. Oh.

(**MILLER** *takes out his gun and takes aim.*)

MILLER. Come on!

HUMPHERY. Here, little lambchop!

BELL. What are you waiting for? Shoot it!

MILLER. You shoot it.

BELL. You're supposed to be the butcher.

MILLER. I know, but…

BELL. Gimme this thing.

(*The* **CYCLOPS** *enters behind and out of sight of the miners.*)

PACKER. I don't think I can watch this.

BELL. So look the other way.

(**PACKER** *turns around, and bumps right into the Cyclops.*)

PACKER. Ooof. (*sees* **CYCLOPS**) WAHHHHHHHH!

HUMPHERY. What? He hasn't even done it yet.

(The miners turn around and see the **CYCLOPS**.*)*

EVERYONE. WAHHHHHHHHH! WAHHHHHHHHH!

CYCLOPS. Are you looking at my eye?!? Are you looking at my eye?!?

EVERYONE. No, no, not at all. (etc. ad lib)

CYCLOPS. A Union Army soldier did this to me in the big one. Any of you boys fight for the Union Army?

SWAN. Shucks, no.

BELL. Shucky dang darn.

CYCLOPS. So you're the boys been killing all my sheepies with those traps.

NOON. Nah! We just now gots here.

CYCLOPS. Where you from?

HUMPHERY. Nayshville.

CYCLOPS. Well, damn! It's good to see some Southern boys. It's been a long time.

(sings)

WELL, I WISH I WERE IN THE LAND OF COTTON
OLD TIMES THERE ARE NOT FORGOTTEN
LOOK AWAY
LOOK AWAY
LOOK AWAY...

(He realizes no one's singing along with him...)

HUMPHERY. "...you stupid Yank."

CYCLOPS. You ain't Southern boys!

EVERYONE. WAHHHHHHHH!!!!

(They all run away.)

PACKER. As the days went by, the snow just got deeper and deeper. And then I realized that maybe the men were losing some hope.

HUMPHERY. Excuse me. I've been doing some thinking, just kinda looking at our thinking, here, and I've come to the conclusion that we're completely FUCKED! Has anybody else made this discovery?

PACKER. But I'm sure this is the right way.

NOON. I don't wanna die. I don't wanna die!

BELL. Yes, the snow is deep.

[MUSIC NO. 09: "LET'S BUILD A SNOWMAN"]

SWAN.

(speak singing)

SOMETIMES THE WORLD IS BLACK
AND TEARS RUN FROM YOUR EYES
AND MAYBE WE'LL ALL GET REALLY SICK
AND MAYBE WE'LL ALL DIE
SO—

(singing)

LET'S BUILD A SNOWMAN
WE CAN MAKE HIM OUR BEST FRIEND
WE CAN NAME HIM TOM
WE CAN NAME HIM BOB
WE CAN MAKE HIM TALL OR
WE CAN MAKE HIM NOT-SO-TALL
SNOWMAN!

HE'LL HAVE A HAPPY FACE
A HAPPY SMILE
A HAPPY POINT OF VIEW
IF YOU BUILD ME A SNOWMAN
I'LL BUILD ONE FOR YOU!

SO, LET'S BUILD A SNOWMAN
WE CAN MAKE HIM OUR BEST FRIEND
WE CAN NAME HIM BOB
OR WE CAN NAME HIM BEOWULF
WE CAN MAKE HIM TALL OR
WE CAN MAKE HIM NOT-SO-TALL
SNOWMAN!

HEY!

(tapdance solo)

> HE'LL HAVE A HAPPY FACE
> A HAPPY SMILE
> A HAPPY POINT-OF-VIEW

MILLER. This fucker's gone completely nuts.

SWAN.

> IF YOU BUILD ME A SNOWMAN
> I'LL BUILD ONE FOR YOU
> SNOWMAN!
> SNOWMAN!
> SNOWMAN!

> (**MILLER** *savagely destroys the snowman* **SWAN** *has made.*)

PACKER. The days were bad, but the nights were worse. All we did was try to keep from freezing. We were all frostbitten and on our last legs, when the butcher suggested we eat our shoes.

HUMPHERY. I'm not eating my fucking shoes!

PACKER. He said the salt in the leather would only hold us over for the night, but we didn't care. It was one more night to stay alive.

MILLER. We're just prolonging the inevitable. We're dying. As in "dead." As in "no more nothing."

BELL. The Lord works in mysterious ways.

MILLER. You realize how stupid that sounds right now, don't you?

BELL. Yes, I do.

SWAN. You know, pretty soon, this whole trip will be behind us and we can look back on it with fond memories.

BELL. What fond memories?!?

SWAN. You have to stay optimistic. This is nothing that a little positive thinking can't help us get through.

MILLER. How the hell can you say that?!? You're frostbitten worse than the rest of us?

SWAN. You never realize what a good time you're having until after it's over.

BELL. Swan, why don't you take a goddamn minute to look around and…

PACKER. Come on, you're just wasting valuable energy.

MILLER AND BELL. Tell him to shut up!

PACKER. Swan, shut up.

SWAN. Oh, you!

(**NOON** *eats some shoe leather, and pulls a fragment of shoestring out of his mouth.* **HUMPHERY** *takes off his hat for the first time ever, and reveals his really wild hair.*)

HUMPHERY. What?

(**THE MINERS** *walk and walk and walk.*)

MILLER. Okay, Packer. What now?

BELL. I can't keep going on like this forever.

NOON. Me neither. We haven't eaten in a week.

BELL. What are we gonna do, Packer?

SWAN. I know what we should do.

NOON. What?

[MUSIC NO. 10: "LET'S BUILD A SNOWMAN REPRISE"]

SWAN.

LET'S BUILD A SNOWMAN
WE CAN MAKE HIM OUR BEST FRIEND

MILLER. *(spoken)* Shut the fuck up, Swan.

SWAN.

WE CAN NAME HIM SHANNON!
SHANNON WILSON BELL

MILLER. *(spoken)* Swan, shut the fuck up!!!

SWAN.

WE CAN MAKE HIM TALL OR
WE CAN MAKE HIM NOT-SO-TALL

(**BELL** *pulls out his gun and shoots* **SWAN.**)

SWAN. Ugh!

(SWAN *dies.*)

NOON. He's dead!

HUMPHERY. Oh, no kidding he's dead! That's his brains all over the snow.

PACKER. He looks so happy.

NOON. He looks like he's gonna sing a song.

[MUSIC NO. 11: "SWAN'S SWAN SONG"]

...

(*The music swells, as if* SWAN *will break into song. He doesn't. Music fizzles out.*)

NOON. Hey, Packer, if we make it out of this, we're gonna turn Bell in, aren't we?

PACKER. I don't know. We'll just figure all that out when we get there.

NOON. If we get there. Hell, we should've gone to California or something.

MILLER. Haven't you ever heard of the Donner Party?

HUMPHERY. Yeah, the Donner Party. They got stuck in the California mountains.

PACKER. They had to eat each other to stay alive.

(PACKER, HUMPHREY, NOON *and* MILLER *all get the same horrible thought at the same horrible moment.*)

HUMPHERY. Heck yeah. Why not?

BELL. Wait a minute, Humphery. You wouldn't even eat your shoes.

HUMPHERY. Well, yeah, but you put your feet in shoes.

MILLER. What do we eat?

HUMPHERY. You're the butcher.

MILLER. Well...yeah, but.... I don't know...

HUMPHERY. (*hands* MILLER *his cleaver*) So, butch.

(MILLER *walks over to* SWAN*'s body and cuts away his clothing to get to the meat.*)

HUMPHERY. Hey, you're cutting into his butt!

MILLER. What kind of piece do you want?

HUMPHERY. Well, not butt!

(They nibble on body parts. **PACKER** *throws up.)*

HUMPHERY. Gross, Packer!

NOON. What about him?

BELL. I don't want any!

MILLER. Fine. You're in Time Out, anyway.

HUMPHERY. Aw, look! You got it on my pants!

*(***PACKER*** *sleeps.)*

[MUSIC NO. 12: "PACKER'S DREAM BALLET"]

*(***PACKER*** *dances a dance of joy with Liane.* **FRENCHY** *arrives and steals Liane.* **PACKER** *fights for Liane.* **FRENCHY** *stabbs* **PACKER.** **PACKER** *falls to the ground.* **FRENCHY** *and* **LIANE** *run off together.)*

*(***PACKER*** *wakes up suddenly, screaming.)*

PACKER. IKE!

(The others wake up suddenly.)

PACKER. Sorry.

HUMPHERY. Is there any more Swan left? I want breakfast.

(The miners walk and walk and walk.)

PACKER. I think we're really close now.

NOON. You know, I have lost count of how many times you've said that. I mean, how long have we been out here? Three weeks?

HUMPHERY. More.

NOON. How far can Breckenridge be?

BELL. Jesus Christ! Don't you idiots get it?!? It's that stupid horse! That's why we're out here freezing and starving to death! Because of his goddamn horse.

PACKER. What?!?

BELL. We're nowhere near Breckenridge. We're way too far south. Don't you remember what's south of Breckenridge? Saguache!

NOON. That's where the trappers were going.

PACKER. You asked me to take you to Breckenridge. That's what I'm trying to do.

BELL. Then why are we so far south?

HUMPHERY. You guys! I just thought of something, too.

PACKER. What?

HUMPHERY. Okay. Now, remember when Swan was building that snowman?

PACKER. Yeah.

HUMPHERY. How the hell did he make that tapping sound with his feet?

NOON. You just now thought of that?

HUMPHERY. That's pretty fucking weird, isn't it?

(**BELL** *and* **HUMPHREY** *fight throughout* **PACKER***'s speech.*)

NOON. You know, Packer, because of you I am never gonna get laid! I'll never get to do it doggy style. Never get to 69. Never get a blow job…(*He continues ad lib under* **PACKER***'s speech.*)

PACKER. Bell's infected leg had finally gotten so bad that he was losing his shpadoinkle. Everybody was, including me. I kept thinking about Liane with those dirty trappers waiting for me to save her. And then I vowed to myself that no matter what, I wouldn't let that happen. That no matter what, I was gonna make it. I knew the first step was to get the men's spirits back up, like Swan would've done.

(**PACKER** *cuts off his moustache.*)

PACKER. You guys. Look. Abe Lincoln.

BELL. Abe Lincoln?!?!?

(**BELL** *attacks* **PACKER.** *All of* **THE MINERS** *collapse in exhaustion.*)

MILLER. You know? It's funny. When we started out on this trip, all I wanted was to be rich. But now, just some food, some warmth… that's all I'm asking for.

[MUSIC NO. 13: "THAT'S ALL I'M ASKING FOR - REPRISE"]

EVERYONE.
THAT'S ALL WE'RE ASKING FOR
THAT'S ALL WE'RE ASKING FOR
FORGET ABOUT THE PIE
WE JUST DON'T WANT TO DIE
WE'VE HAD SOME ROTTEN LUCK
WE CAN'T TAKE IT ANY MORE
WE DON'T CARE IF WE'RE FOREVER POOR
THAT'S ALL WE'RE ASKING FOR

HUMPHERY. So cold… Can't move… Can't feel… Can't make complete sentences. We have to eat something.

MILLER. Maybe we should sacrifice somebody.

NOON. He's right. If one of us dies, the others can live.

HUMPHERY. It should be Bell. He killed Swan. It's only fair.

MILLER. I agree.

BELL. You should kill him. He's the one who got us into this.

PACKER. Whoa. Whoa. Wait a minute. We're almost up over this last ridge. We can probably see a long ways from there.

NOON. We can't do it, Packer. We can't even stand up.

PACKER. I'll go. You guys watch the fire. And nobody eat anybody!

(*INSERT: map* – **PACKER** *goes off looking for food.*)

(**PACKER** *returns. All the miners are dead.*)

PACKER. Okay, you guys, I was wrong about the ridge, but… *(sees the massacre)* What are you guys doing?

BELL. Yeah, they were gonna kill me. After you left, they attacked me, so I had to defend myself. Looks like it's survival of the strongest, eh, Packer? Maybe it's for the best. I mean, now we have enough meat to last us for weeks. Hell, we may even make it till summer. Yes, sir, the Lord works in mysterious ways. We can say we lost these boys, bury the bodies, and no one will ever know. I can open my church and you can build your ranch.

PACKER. I think we should probably just go tell somebody. You know? I mean, if it was in self-defense –

BELL. Don't be stupid, man! Nobody will believe this. Don't forget, you ate Swan, too. If anybody finds out about any of this, they'll hang us both.

PACKER. Why? You killed them.

BELL. That's not how I remember it. I'm not about to let some ignorant poke ruin my chance of becoming a priest!

PACKER. You know what, Bell? I think you've really lost it. And I don't think you killed these guys in self defense, either. I think you just killed them. And I'm telling.

BELL. You're not telling anybody anything ever again!

(**PACKER** *kills* **BELL**)

[MUSIC NO. 14: "PACKER'S LAMENT"]

Why do I...

(**PACKER,** *spent, exhausted, and sings one or two words, when suddenly...*)

(**BELL** *screams and attacks* **PACKER** *again.*)

(**PACKER** *kills* **BELL** *again.*)

[MUSIC NO. 15: "PACKER'S LAMENT - REPRISE"]

I...

(**PACKER,** *doesn't even get to the first word when...*)

(**BELL** *screams and attacks* **PACKER** *yet again.*)

(**PACKER** *kills* **BELL** *yet again.*)

(*This time,* **PACKER** *pokes* **BELL** *and tries to fake him out, but* **BELL** *stays dead.* **PACKER** *walks away.*)

PACKER. The snowstorms didn't let up, so I stayed in that camp for weeks living off the bodies of the others. I knew right then no one would believe what happened. I made my way to an Indian agency and they just fixed me up and sent me to the nearest town. I told everyone that I didn't know where the others were, that I'd lost them, but then...

(SIGN: *"Saguache, Colorado 1874"*)

(*Enter* **SHERIFF** *of Saguache.*)

SHERIFF. Alferd Packer? I'm the Sheriff of Saguache. Some people are getting mighty suspicious of you.

PACKER. Me?

SHERIFF. Well, the rest of your party haven't shown up yet.

PACKER. Yeah?

SHERIFF. I'm gonna put together a search party and I'd like you to come along and show us where you last saw them.

PACKER. I can't. See, I have to get back to Utah and try to find my...

SHERIFF. Back to Utah?!? What if those people are still up there struggling for their lives?

PACKER. Okay. I'll go.

SHERIFF. All right. Meet me in my office at sunrise. You know what they say about sunrise, don't you?

(**SHERIFF** *nods knowingly, then exits.* **PACKER** *looks after him, clueless.*)

(**LIANE** *enters.*)

PACKER. Liane!!!

(**THE TRAPPERS** *enter.* **LIANE** *and* **FRENCHY** *are all over each other.*)

FRENCHY. Well, don't you look sharp! What'cha doing here in Saguache? I thought you were headed to Breckenridge.

PACKER. This is my horse!

FRENCHY. She just followed me here.

PACKER. She's letting you ride her. Come here, girl!

FRENCHY. Tell ya what. I'll give you eight dollars for her.

PACKER. Keep your money.

> (**PACKER** *walks off, dejected. He enters the saloon.* **THE TRAPPERS** *follow him in. Everyone is now in the Saloon.*)

PACKER. At that moment, I realized Liane hadn't been stolen. She'd left me. For him!

FRENCHY. So, they tell me you lost the rest of your party! Kinda misplaced them, did ya? Just kinda hanging back, having a little drinky-poo, huh?

PACKER. I'm having a drinky-poo. Leave me alone.

FRENCHY. Not only did I get here two months ahead of you, Packer, but I came back with everyone I started with.

PACKER. Tell me something, Frenchy. How does it feel to be riding my horse?

FRENCHY. Come off it, Packer. Everyone in this town has ridden your horse.

> (**PACKER** *punches* **FRENCHY.**)

FRENCHY. You're gonna pay for that, digger.

> (**SHERIFF** *of Saguache enters.*)

SHERIFF. Packer? Packer! You lied. They found the bodies up on Slumgolian Pass. They were eaten! I'm taking you downtown, cannibal!

CYCLOPS. You little bastard! Now you must die!

PACKER. Oh, fuck.

> (*Everyone beats the crap out of* **PACKER.**)

FRENCHY. NO! WAIT! He's mine. I'm going to show you what it means to be a trapper.

> (*Everyone steps away from* **PACKER. PACKER** *lies on the floor, bruised.*)

(**PACKER** *hears the* **CHIEF***'s voice.*)

CHIEF. *(voice over)* Remember what you learned, Packer-san. Don't be such a wimp.

(*With much difficulty,* **PACKER** *stands and faces* **FRENCHY***.*)

PACKER. You dirty so-and-so, horsey-snatching little…

(*They fight.* **PACKER** *pummels* **FRENCHY** *in the crotch.* **FRENCHY** *drops to his knees.* **PACKER** *grabs* **FRENCHY** *in a head-lock.*)

PACKER. Okay, nobody move, or else…*(thinks quickly)* …I'll eat this guy right in front of you.

FRENCHY. *(in a high-pitched voice)* He's serious, man! Don't move!

SHERIFF. He is a cannibal!

(**PACKER** *throws* **FRENCHY** *to the ground then runs off.*)

FRENCHY. Don't just stand there! Go get him!

SHERIFF. Let's go get him!

(*A huge chase scene ensues. Eventually,* **PACKER** *runs away from the group.*)

(**PACKER** *sees* **LIANE***. He rushes up to her. She turns her back on him and farts at him.*)

(*Heartbroken,* **PACKER** *runs away.*)

PACKER. And I ran and I ran and I ran just as fast as I possibly could.

POLLY. But you got away, right?

PACKER. Yeah, but I would've been better off just letting those people catch me and kill me.

POLLY. Why?

PACKER. I went to Wyoming.

POLLY. Oh, God, how horrible!

PACKER. I managed to hide out there for a while, but they caught up with me, brought me back, and now I don't know what's gonna happen.

POLLY. You'll be fine, I promise. And I'll be with the whole time. You'll see, Alferd. There won't be a hanging day.

PACKER. Gee, that made me feel better. You know, I think maybe there is hope.

(SIGN: *"Hanging Day"*)

(**POLLY** *exits.*)

(**MILLS** *and* **SHERIFF** *enter.*)

MR. MILLS. I know that today will be a day that goes down in history as the day in which justice was truly served. Now let's hang the bastard!

SHERIFF. Come on, Packer. It's time for the show.

PACKER. Wait. Did you see that lady that's been around here?

SHERIFF. Polly Pry? She went back to Denver.

PACKER. Denver?

SHERIFF. Yeah. She works for the Denver Post. Didn't you know that? Douchebag.

[MUSIC NO. 16: "HANG THE BASTARD"]

TOWNSFOLK.

HANG THE BASTARD
HANG HIM HIGH
HOIST HIS BODY TO THE SKY
IT'S AS NICE AS A DAY CAN BE
WON'T YOU COME TO THE HANGING WITH ME?

HANG THE BASTARD
HANG HIM HIGH
HOIST HIS BODY TO THE SKY
IT'S AS NICE AS A DAY CAN BE
WON'T YOU COME TO THE HANGING WITH ME

HANG THE BASTARD
HANG HIM WELL
SEND HIS SORRY SOUL TO HELL
WHEN HIS NECKBONE SNAPS WE'LL KNOW
THAT THE CANNIBAL WON'T BE KILLING ANYMORE

HIS FACE WILL TURN RED
THEN PURPLE, THEN BLUE
WE'LL WATCH FROM HERE TO GET A GOOD VIEW
AND WHEN HIS EYES BULGE OUT WE'LL KNOW
IT'S THE END OF HIM AND THE END OF THE SHOW

SO, HANG THE BASTARD
HANG HIM WITH CHEER
WE'LL MAKE SOME HOT DOGS
AND DRINK A FEW BEERS
AND WHEN HIS TONGUE ROLLS OUT WE'LL KNOW
IT'S THE END OF THE SHOW AND WE ALL CAN GO HOME

BUT NOT TILL WE HANG THE BASTARD
HANG HIM HERE
THE MOST EXCITING THING
THIS TOWN HAS SEEN IN YEARS
WHEN HIS BODY STOPS JERKING WE'LL KNOW
IT'S THE END OF HIM
IT'S THE END OF HIM
IT'S THE END OF HIM
AND THE END OF THE SHOW

COWBELL SOLO!

SO, HANG THE BASTARD
HANG HIM HIGH
KISS HIS GUILTY BUTT GOODBYE
IT'S AS NICE AS A DAY CAN BE
WON'T YOU COME TO THE HANGING WITH ME?

HIS FACE WILL POP ALL OVER HIS HEAD
WE'LL TICKLE HIS ARMPITS TO MAKE SURE HE'S DEAD
AND WHEN HIS TONGUE ROLLS OUT WE'LL KNOW
IT'S THE END OF HIM AND WE ALL CAN GO HOME

BUT – NOT – TILL – WE –
HANG THE BASTARD
HANG HIM HIGH
HOIST HIS BODY TO THE SKY
AND WHEN HIS BODY STOPS JERKING WE'LL KNOW
IT'S THE END OF HIM
IT'S THE END OF HIM

IT'S THE END OF HIM

NOW GET ON WITH THE SHOW—

HURRAY!

(**PACKER** *stands with a noose around his neck. Everyone is gathered to watch the hanging.*)

SHERIFF. Alferd Packer, do you have any last words?

PACKER. Yes, I do.

CROWD. Aw!

SHERIFF. All right. Make it snappy.

PACKER. Probably the most important thing is that when things get really bad and the world looks its darkest, you just have to throw up your hands and say, "Well, all right." Cuz it's probably gonna get a whole hell of a lot worse.

SHERIFF. Jolly good speech! Now let's get on with the hanging.

CROWD. Hurray!

SHERIFF. Release the floor!

PACKER. *(his last words:)* Shpadoinkle!

(**POLLY** *rushes on riding Liane.*)

POLLY. WAIT!! WAIT!! Move it! Wait! This is a Stay of Execution ordered by the Governor.

SHERIFF. What? Why?

POLLY. The events that this man is being hung for took place before Colorado was made into a state. This was all Ute Indian Reservation. Packer cannot legally be tried under state law.

MR. MILLS. I'm afraid you're out of line, Miss Pry.

POLLY. No, Mr. Mills, it's you who's out of line, since you knew about this the entire trial.

MR. MILLS. Polly, why are you doing this?!?

POLLY. Because I've learned something, about helping people instead of manipulating them.

PACKER. Does this mean I'm not going to die today?

POLLY. Yes! Yes, Alferd, it does!

PACKER. But why did you go to all this trouble?

POLLY. Do you want to know why?

PACKER. Yes.

[MUSIC NO. 17: "WHEN I WAS ON TOP OF YOU - REPRISE"]

POLLY.
YOUR EYES
YOUR SMILE
MAKE MY LITTLE LIFE WORTHWHILE
THERE'S NOWHERE I'D RATHER BE
IF YOU WERE ON TOP OF—

(**FRENCHY** *pulls the two lovers apart.*)

FRENCHY. What the hell do you think you're doing here, lady? These people came to see some good violence, and by golly they're gonna see some.

CROWD. Yeah!

FRENCHY. Die, Cheezmo.

PACKER. Wait!

(**FRENCHY** *pulls the lever and* **PACKER** *hangs.*)

(**CHIEF** *rushes on and cuts the noose.* **PACKER** *falls safely to the ground.*)

FRENCHY. Hey, you can't do that, jerky.

CHIEF. You are a bad, bad person! Ya!!!

(**CHIEF** *chases* **FRENCHY** *offstage.*)

(*SOUND:* **CHIEF** *lopping off* **FRENCHY**'s *head, offstage.*)

FRENCHY. Ow.

(**CHIEF** *comes back onstage with* **FRENCHY**'s *head.*)

PACKER. Chief, how did you get here?

CHIEF. Your friend told me you needed help.

PACKER. Liane!

POLLY. I found her for you, Alferd.

PACKER. Here, girl!

(**LIANE** *turns her back on* **PACKER** *and farts at him…*)

POLLY. I'll go get her.

PACKER. No. I don't need her any more. Hey, Chief, you want a horse?

CHIEF. You don't want the horse?

PACKER. No. I think I know what I want now. Someone who really cares about me.

POLLY. There's an appeal case to work on, Alferd. I have to go back to Denver. But I'll be back up tomorrow.

PACKER. Gosh, how can I ever repay you?

POLLY. You already have, Alferd! You already have!

TINY TIM. God bless us, every one!

[MUSIC NO. 18: "SHPADOINKLE DAY - REPRISE"]

POLLY.
THE SKY IS BLUE
AND ALL THE LEAVES ARE GREEN

PACKER.
MY HEART'S AS FULL AS A BAKED POTATO
BOTH:
I'M SURE YOU KNOW EXACTLY WHAT I MEAN
WHEN I SAY IT'S A SHPADOINKLE DAY

ALL.
WHEN WE SAY IT'S A SHPADOINKLE DAY!!!

(*SIGN: "Due to the continued efforts of Polly Pry, Alferd Packer was eventually released from prison in 1901."*)

(*Suddenly,* **BELL** *jumps out, all bloody and not-yet-dead. Everyone screams and runs offstage.*)

[MUSIC NO. 19: "CURTAIN CALL"]

(*SIGN: "Due to the graphic nature of this play it should not have been watched by young children."*)

www.ingramcontent.com/pod-product-compliance
Lightning Source LLC
Chambersburg PA
CBHW071205120325
23390CB00008B/298